B is for Bear

Marc Richard

DEDICATION

For my Crew: Marla Alvather, Gayle Armstrong, David Berg, Curtis Bushart, Marshall Clowers, Ari Cohen, Steve Cohen, Chris Coleman, Kelly Connerton, Rhonda Corson, Alex Cunningham, Johannes Debler, Tony Dodds, Tere Fredericks,Tam French, Emily G., Anne Marie Kaczorowksi, Larry Marek, Norma Miles, Bob Newman, Quentin Norman, Crystal Organ, Caleb Orion, Elizabeth Peacock, NickPerry, Martha Reed, Steve Roberts, Kym Russell, Michelle Sime, Dawn Taylor, Virna Thibault, Jill Thibodeau, Justin Tyler, Craig Ware, Ron Wells, Papa Woodie, Art, Bri, Lori, Melissa, Pam, Pati, Raymond, Rich, and Teddy. Thank you for making this possible.

And as always thank you to the Queen of the Dance Floor, Aisha Hashmi.

Contents

1. That's Amore!

The lights beaming off the disco ball played tricks with the eye as they danced through Jimmy DiFreno's chest hair. He was quite proud of his chest hair. It was part of his culture to be proud of his chest hair.

He wasn't much to look at. He didn't have the classic chiseled looks of a Rudy Valentino or an Antonio Sabato Jr. You know, looks that could make the ladies swoon while simultaneously being a silent killer. No, he had the stereotypical looks of a James Gandolfini: Six-foot-two, two hundred seventy-five pounds, give or take. He knew that if he kept eating the way he did, he would most likely end up like the late great Gandolfini, but boy, did he love his *gabagool*. And spaghetti and meatballs. And *pasta fazool*. And pie. You get the picture. Not that he wasn't a good-looking guy in his own way; it was just hard to get people to believe that he wasn't in the mob with his appearance being the way it was. I mean, he *was* in the mob, in fact, he was the Don; I'm just saying he couldn't hide the fact.

He usually dressed up very nicely in Armani suits, but when it came time to leave the cozy confines of his office in the back and get down on the dance floor of his own night club, Stella, he donned a pair of jeans and a button-down shirt, unbuttoned halfway, so that his marvelous chest hair could rustle like dried leaves in the wind. He also wore a gold chain, which further accented said chest hair and Italian heritage.

He was at Stella practically every day; however, he only got out on the dance floor a couple nights a week. He usually spent most of his time in the back room, doing books, or other some other business. Most of which was not exactly on the up and up. Stella was a front for a more lucrative, and less tax-collectible, business. Obviously. Every decent mafia crew had several legitimate businesses: laundromats, restaurants, night clubs, assassins-for-hire, birthday clowns, and on and on. A mob without a front to hide behind was like a freight train carrying a cargo of drugs and running over a beautiful Mexican woman who looked an awful lot like Salma Hayek. Not sure what that means? Jimmy did.

He often got mistaken for a bear. No, not a real bear, since that would be weird to have a real bear in a club. Keep up, dummies. Since he was hairy, and large, and (some may even say) cuddly, occasionally other men would hit on him. He had an ironic vibe about him that most of the overly macho men of the bear persuasion were guilty of affecting. Like Freddie Mercury or Rob Halford, that kind of thing. It didn't happen too often, since this wasn't a gay club. But it happened often enough. And when it did, he would put on airs like it offended him. In reality, though, he felt honored. Not that he'd ever have sex with them; he didn't swing that way. Unless it came to Joe.

Most everyone in the mafia, and especially the Dons, had a little *goomah* on the side. A Don without a *goomah* was like a bald man picking up spare change. So, that's why it came as a shock to Jimmy that his wife Charlene had no clue. There was a possibility that she knew and just chose to never bring it up, but he highly doubted it. Charlene's father was Don Figarazzi. The Don of the very famous Figarazzi family. The funny thing was, his name was also Don.

Anyway, when he got to the age that he was "too old for this crap", he handed the reigns to Jimmy. Sadly, he had no sons of his own, and since Charlene was the apple of Don's eye, it was his decision to give Jimmy the job. That way, his grandson could continue when he was old enough. This pissed off a lot of actual family members, including his brother Don, his nephew Donald, and his three cousins, Don, Don, and Timmy, but Don's decision was Don's decision, and so it stood.

Jimmy's father-in-law knew that he had a *goomah* on the side; it didn't really bother him. It wasn't Don's wrath that concerned him. It was Charlene's. If she found out, not only would she cut his balls off, but she would also convince her father to have him taken out. Even though Jimmy was Don, Don was still the Don of the Don, and there were plenty of actual Figarazzi's that would have been more than happy to do the job.

Don Figarazzi would have killed him if he knew just who Jimmy was fooling around on Charlene with: His best buddy Joe. The Mafia community frowns upon homosexuality. It's a sign of weakness. In Italian dialect they call it a *fanook*, and Jimmy most definitely wasn't one.

Now Joe, he wasn't so sure about, but really, who was he to cast aspersions? Joe was his capo, his best friend, and sometimes, his lover. That didn't make him gay, right?

Right?

You see, Joe saved Jimmy's ass in 'Nam. Joe nursed his dog to health when he didn't have a paw to stand on. Joe gave him a place to stay when he got out of the army and had no place to go. Joe rescued his mother from a burning building. He and Joe opened their first hot dog stand together, back when they were just kiddies in Brooklyn. Joe tipped him off on some winning lottery numbers. Joe gave him grape soda when he needed a fine carbonated beverage. All this you may already know; I'm not sure how much Jimmy has divulged to you. And tonight, he got himself a nice hummer in the bathroom. Not the truck, although he had one of those as well. And that would not fit in the bathroom. By hummer, I meant he got his dick sucked by Joe. Oh? I didn't have to explain that? You understood that already by the context? My bad.

Anyway, enough about Joe for now. The evening at Stella was at full swing, but Jimmy had his fair share of paperwork to do before he went home.

2. Meet the DiFrenzos

It was ten o'clock when Jimmy barged in. "Honey, I'm home!" he liked to shout, just like old Mr. Gleason used to do. And Charlene usually greeted him with a warm embrace at the front door. However, Charlene was not in the mood for pleasantries. Despite the disheveled look she was sporting at the moment, she was still beautiful: tall, thin, long dark hair, gorgeous brown eyes he could swim in when he remembered to bring his trunks, and a usual look of adoration on her face. But not tonight.

"What's wrong, Charl?" he asked.

"Gimme the controller, jerk!" he heard his son call from the other room.

"That," Charlene answered.

"Who's he talking to?"

She sighed. "Your sister dropped her daughter off. It's been like this all day."

"What, the fightin'? Usually they get along."

"I think your niece is sick or something. She seems overtired, which has been setting Jimmy Junior off every five minutes."

"Don't worry," Jimmy said, and gave her a kiss on her forehead, "I'll straighten this out."

"Hey kids!" Charlene heard Senior say all friendly, like some big, dumb clown.

"Hey pop," Junior said.

"Hey Uncle Jim," his niece said.

Then the fighting continued.

"I said, gimme that!"

"Woah, woah, woah. The hell is goin' on?"

"She's been hogging the game," Junior said.

"So? She's your guest. And it's past ten. Get to bed.

"But daaaad..."

"But daaaad nothing. I'll be up to kiss you goodnight in a minute. Go on. Git."

He turned to his niece. "Your ma comin' to pick you up tonight?"

"Yeah, sometime," she answered.

"The whore," he muttered.

"What, Uncle Jim?"

"I said your mother is a lovely woman. Go on up to the guest room till your ma comes."

"Okay," she said, and headed upstairs.

He went back into the kitchen. "You all

right?" he asked.

"Yeah, just tired. Kids."

"You sure nothing else is on your mind?" He got paranoid every time he had relations with Joe, and tonight, as you know, was one of those nights. Did she know something?

"No. Just the kids. Why?"

He kissed her on the forehead again. "No reason. I'm gonna go say goodnight to little Jim."

"Kiss him for me too," said Charlene. "I'd do it myself, but I've had more than enough for one evening."

"Sure thing."

He knocked gently on his son's bedroom door, even though it was open a crack, like it always was. There he was, in his bed fast asleep. The day must have wiped him out.

Little Jimmy was eleven. Tonight was a bad example of the way the boy usually was. He was really a good kid. So well-behaved. And smart; he made the honor roll every quarter. He loved that little rugrat with all his soul, and hoped to God that he didn't follow in his old man's footsteps. Buuuutt, if he *did* follow in his old man's footsteps, Jimmy Sr. would be quite proud indeed. Just sayin'. He knew what the first signs would be. He would get a mouth on him. A lot of those in the family, they had kids with smart mouths, especially the boys. That's when it all would start, the downhill slide. They went straight from mouthing off to stealing candy from the corner store, right to gunning down rival families in the course of a year or two. Okay, so Jimmy was a little bit jealous. He shouldn't be; like I said, he was proud of Little Jimmy. But there was a part deep down that kinda wished he'd come home early from school for calling the teacher a twat-waffle or something.

The boy rolled over, and the light from the night-light lit his face up like a little cherub in a painting. His eyes were open.

"Dad?" he asked.

"Yeah?" he answered.

"I love you."

"I love you too, Jim. Very much." He brushed his son's hair out of his eyes and gave him a kiss on the cheek. "Good night, son."

"Good night."

Jimmy Senior turned to leave.

"Dad?"

"Yes?"

"I got somethin' to confess."

"I'm all ears."

"I got sent home from school today."

"What? Why?"

"I called the lunch lady a twat-waffle."

Lunch lady? Was that as good as a teacher? Yes, he was pretty sure it was.

"Shhh. Go to sleep, son," he said, and left the room.

Charlene was sitting at the kitchen table.

"Honey, you look beat. Why don't you head on up to bed?"

"Yeah, I suppose I should. Wanna come up with me? Got time for some lovey-lovey?"

"Not tonight, Charl. Too tired. I'm gonna do the dishes. Go on to bed, I'll be up in a bit."

She gave him a long kiss on his lips. "Night, honey. I love you. Thanks for doing the dishes."

"You're welcome. Love you too. Night, Charl."

And as he scrubbed the pots and pans, he couldn't help but smile, beaming.

"Lunch lady," he said. "How do ya like that?"

3. The Twat-Waffle Diaries

The following day was fairly uneventful. Jimmy spent most of it in his office, balancing the books. If anyone had told him that most of his work as a boss would involve paperwork, he probably would have passed on the whole thing. He missed the action of being a capo, or even a soldier. Sure, the pay was nice, but whereas soldiers often suffered from gunshot wounds, he was suffering from boredom, which was ten times worse. He called a meeting just to keep from pulling his own hair out, and was mostly about things like Why do you guys keep coming up light with the money, and We need to kill more people, and things of that nature. You know, the typical. You've all seen the movies. Still, he'd much rather be in the office than have to go through what Charlene was doing at the moment.

She sat across the desk from the school principal. The look of disdain he gave her was something Jimmy would have smacked him in the mouth for, if he were here instead of her. That's why she was glad it was her here instead of him. Jim had a hard time keeping his cool with people criticizing his son. By being angry at the principal, it was a misdirected anger, she reminded herself, when it should be aimed toward that little boy that was waiting in the hallway, the one that had called the lunch lady names.

"Listen, Mrs. DiFrenzo, Jimmy really is a good boy. He's one of the top students in his class, as you probably already know. If he just applied himself, and kept out of mischief, he could go really far in this world."

"Thank you," answered Charlene.

"But once in a while, he does things that we don't see in other children."

"Like calling the lunch lady a twat-waffle?" she asked.

"No, not at all. Had he called his teacher a twat-waffle, I would have suspended him instead of just sending him home. Miss Bean, the lunch lady, well, everyone calls her twat-waffle. You see, she has an unfortunate anatomical issue that, well, is unfortunate."

"I see."

"But that's neither here nor there," the principal said. "No, I'm afraid Jimmy's issues go much deeper than name calling."

"Like?"

"Like telling a boy he was going to have him whacked."

"He what, now?" she asked.

"He told a boy he was going to have him whacked. To be fair, Jimmy was just defending himself, as the boy has been known to be a bully. But when he used a word like *whacked*, well, given the circumstances with your family situation and all, the boy is now in fear of his life."

She glared at him, but he didn't notice.

"And the other day, we thought we'd bring back show and tell. I mean, nobody's too old for show and tell, right? Mrs. DiFrenzo, your boy brought a gun to school as his presentation. It was then we realized that maybe you *can* be too old for show and tell."

"He what?"

"He brought a gun to school. To be fair, the gun was not loaded, and he was only trying to teach the kids gun safety. But I don't think at his age he has any authority to teach anyone about gun safety. And given the circumstances with your family situation and all, with his father being who he is, and your father being who he is..."

"What do you mean by *that*?" she just about shouted.

The principal's eyes widened as his life flashed before him. You had to choose your words properly when dealing with, well, you know.

"Uh, er, nothing. I'm sorry. Forget I said anything, okay? *Please?*"

She was thinking they should have enrolled him in a private Catholic school. The faculty there were used to dealing with Mafiosi, and this wouldn't have been a big deal. In fact, they probably would have offered her some coffee when she went into the office. Charlene had not gotten offered coffee. Perhaps it was best they look into St. Mark's. Maybe her husband was right, maybe public school wasn't the right fit for them.

"Yeah," answered Charlene. "All right. Water under the bridge." She got up to leave. "And thank you for your time, Bob," she said as she shook his hand. "My husband and I will have a long talk with Junior. I think there will be some major changes coming."

He grinned. Perhaps they would take him out of his school after all. That would certainly be a lot of weight off of his shoulders. "It was nice to see you again, Charlene," he said, as she headed toward the door.

"Please," she said, "call me Mrs. DiFrenzo."

And with that, she left his office and marched straight toward her boy waiting in the hallway.

"How did it go in there?" he asked.

"You brought a *gun* to school? *Seriously?*"

"It's never too early to learn about gun safety, mom."

"You can't bring a gun to school. These days, with all the school shootings? What the hell is wrong with you?"

"I guess I..."

"And telling a boy you would have a hit taken out on him?"

"I hate it here, mom. I hate *everyone* here. And I think my exact phrasing was that I would have him whacked."

"You can't say that!" she yelled. "Especially given the circumstances with our family situation and all."

"Just what is our situation, mom?"

"Never mind," she said. "There is no situation."

"When am I finally going to learn the truth about what dad does, and what grandpa did?"

"Your dad owns a club. That's it. It's no secret."

"Yeah, but that's not all he does, is it?"

She sighed, and looked at her watch. It was still early.

"Come on," she said, "let's go get some breakfast. I'll call your dad and he can meet us at IHOP and we can talk about alternative schooling options. Whaddaya say?"

"Yes! I'm starving," he answered. "I could sure go for some waffles."

4. Blondie

Her name was Marguerite but everyone called her Blondie. A spoiled little rich bitch. That was how others described her, and to her that seemed accurate and fair. She *was* a spoiled little rich bitch. There wasn't a moment in her seventeen years of life where she had wanted for anything. Everything she had ever asked for, she got. And then some. Her father had been dead for years now, murdered, and her mother tried getting her though the grieving process. Not with love and understanding, but opting for the easier way of parenting for those with money: showering her with gifts.

She was a beautiful girl with big blue eyes, long blond hair, and a figure to die for. For a teenager she was well-developed. I will not go into specifics, I am not a pervert, but let's just leave it at she was very attractive. She could have any boy she wanted, but she didn't want boys. Or girls. No, what turned her on was danger.

Years ago, the tedium of spoiled rich bitch life had gotten to her, and that's when she started breaking into homes. She had never stolen or taken anything from anyone, since she already had everything she wanted. The excitement was in the unlawful entry. It was just something fun to do, to see if she could get away with it. She was good at it, too, only getting caught one time out of the hundred homes she had broken into. The owners had caught her sleeping in their bed, and were about to call the police when she prattled on with her well-rehearsed story about being a homeless orphan with no place to go. They felt sorry for her, fed her some porridge, and offered to adopt her. The only caveat, they told her, was that once in a while they would call upon her to do some favors for her new adopted father of the intimate variety, since his wife was a frigid woman. By the time the mother-to-be explained the wonders of Hershey's chocolate syrup, she had bolted out the front door, and they would never see her again. Weirdos.

This little incident didn't stop her from

breaking into homes, however. Quite the contrary, in fact. It added a little more excitement to the whole deal. I mean, she knew deep down there was always a possibility of getting caught, but now that it had happened, it made it that much more real. And now, here she was, standing in back of a house that belonged to the biggest mob family in the city. This was it. The pinnacle of her breaking and entering days had finally come.

The DiFrenzos' home was like a fortress. Fully equipped with a state-of-the-art security system and the best locking mechanisms for doors and windows money could buy, and being who he was, Jimmy had spared no expense in keeping his family safe. Nothing in the world was more important than the well-being of his wife and kid.

She got past all that by throwing a rock through a rear window. This set the alarm off, but by this point, she was quite the professional. Within seconds, she had the alarm disarmed.

Wow, this was the life. *Just look at this place,* she thought. Sure, her family had money, but nothing at all like this. So this is what blood money bought you. The biggest house on the block, with all the nicest things. Everything was so state-of-the-art, so excessive. She loved it. However, right now she had something in her eye which she was hoping wasn't glass.

She found her way to the bathroom. One of many, she was certain. Rich people always felt the need to have more bathrooms in their homes than they had people living there. Her own family was no exception with five. She wasn't sure why this was the case. It was just more to clean. Although, let's be real, her family cleaned nothing. That's what they had the Guatemalan maid for. Sure, they could have used a service like Happy Maids, but to have a true Guatemalan, that really screamed something about their status.

She looked in the mirror and examined her eye. An eyelash had gotten in it. This happened frequently, as she had such long, gorgeous eyelashes. She gave her eyeball a swipe with the tip of her finger and removed the offensive lash.

Now her eye felt irritated. She looked in the medicine cabinet for some Clear Eyes or something. Nothing there to help her eye, but there were some OxyContin she pocketed for later.

She had never in her life seen a triple vanity, but the DiFrenzos had one, each with their own sets of drawers. All stenciled with their names: Jim Sr., Charlene, Jim Jr. Wasn't that just darling? She opened the drawer that belonged to Jim Jr. Nothing in it but a Spongebob toy and a bottle of hair gel, medium crisp. In Charlene's drawers she found the typical woman stuff: emergency makeup, curling iron, straightening iron, and hair gel, low crisp. Jim Senior's drawers held nothing but seventy-two types of aftershave and a bottle of hair gel, EXXXTreme Crisp. She tossed all three bottles of hair gel on the floor in a moment of frustration. Nothing for her eye. Oh well, the irritation should go away in a little bit; it was time to explore some more.

Suddenly hungry, she went to the kitchen to see if they had anything good to eat. What a massive kitchen it was! And so fancy. Marble counter tops, marble floors, a Viking stove, Sub-Zero refrigerator, all the best equipment. And so clean! There wasn't a cutting board in the sink, no signs of spillage on the stove. She would bet money on them getting takeout all the time. She knew that when someone had a kitchen this nice, they rarely used it, but perhaps there was something in the fridge anyway.

Not much, apparently. Beer, white wine, lots

of condiments, some sandwich meat. Three kinds of capicola! She opened the plastic bag with the first variety in it. Spicy capicola. She'd never had the spicy kind. Wooh! Too hot. She threw the bag of meat across the room. In the second bag was sweet capicola. Almost *too* sweet, though. It tasted like it was honey-cured, then more honey poured over it when it finished curing. Too much. She threw that bag across the room, too. She opened the third bag to taste. That was just right, with the proper blend of spicy and sweet. Finding some bread in the box on the counter, she decided to fix a sandwich.

Wonder what's on tv? Blondie asked herself. She flopped down on the beanbag chair in the corner like a three-hundred-pound octopus. A slight tear in the bag allowed the beans to spew out all across the room. This chair was too soft. She tried the recliner. Most likely that belonged to Jimmy DiFrenzo himself; most men of his ilk had their own special chairs that they allowed no one else to sit in. It looked comfortable, but sitting in it was a different story. Too hard. It had that feel that some furniture gets before you break it in. Since she figured Jimmy had spent a lot of time in front of the tube, and his massive frame would break in a chair in no time, it must have been new. She was more of a couch girl, anyway, and she sauntered on over to the sofa and got herself comfy. It felt just right. It was so comfortable, in fact, that for the first time in her life, she considered stealing something. Her couch at home was too formal—okay to sit in, but not cushy enough to lie down on. Unfortunately, her mother just loved the couch, and all their guests just loved the couch, and there was no way she could swap it out and have people not notice. Also, she couldn't move a couch by herself. No, this was a couch dream, and couch dreams were for sissies and baseball players, for Christmas carol crooners and turkey stuffers.

She turned on the tv but instead of happily choosing a program, she felt irritated. No Roku, no Amazon Fire Stick, just straight cable. She'd heard of cable tv before, but had never witnessed it. Such an antique concept. It should have been charming that these people were holding onto old tradition, but it was annoying as hell to her. She flipped through the channels, discouraged that she had to deal with what was on right at that moment instead of being able to pick any show she wanted. How disturbing. It made little sense. They were rich. Why in the world would they... oh well. It didn't matter. She checked her cell phone for the time. Ten o'clock. The DiFrenzos wouldn't be home for a while yet, not until Junior got out of school, anyway.

She flipped through the channels till she stumbled upon *The People's Court*. Seemed kind of interesting. She took a bite of her sandwich. The combination of Wonder Bread and mayonnaise stuck to the roof of her mouth. She needed something to wash it down with. *May as well help myself to a beer or three,* she thought. Although she liked to consider herself a rebel, she really wasn't much of a drinker, and by the time she'd finished her third beer, she was fast asleep on the couch.

5. Who's the Bimbo?

After a nice breakfast at IHOP, the DiFrenzos all headed home, Charlene and Junior in her Hummer, and Jimmy in his. Charlene got herself and Junior out of her vehicle, and headed for the front door when Jimmy got out of his own vehicle and yelled, "Wait!"

She turned to her husband, and he shook his head. "Somethin's not right here," he said.

"What's not right here?"

"Look. Right through the livin' room window. Notice somethin'?"

"What am I noticing?" she asked.

"You don't see it? You left the fuckin' tv on again. How many times, Charl? How many times have I had to tell you that electricity costs money and money don't grow on bushes and whatnot?"

"Three hundred," she said. "But it wasn't

me."

"Junior, how many times have I told you that money don't grow on bushes and whatnot?"

"Five hundred," he said. "But it wasn't me."

"Well," said Jimmy, "if it weren't you, and it weren't *you*, then who was it? Did someone break into our unbreakable house and turn the tv on?"

"That's crazy," Charlene said.

"Preposterous," Junior echoed with a different word. He had obviously been spending a lot of time with his new thesaurus.

"Ludicrous," said Jimmy, who had also glanced occasionally at the thesaurus.

"There's no need to bring his name into this," said Charlene, who was feeling bad that she'd only used a word with two syllables.

"Hmm," said Jimmy. "Must be a ghost or somethin'. Come on, let's go in, I'm hungry."

"Hungry?" Charlene asked. "You just ate a huge breakfast."

"Yeah, but you know what they say about pancakes. Eat as much as you want, in an hour or so you'll be hungry again."

Charlene never heard this expression. Pancakes always made her feel like she ate more of them than she actually did.

Jimmy shouted from the kitchen. "Hey, you wanna sandwich?"

"Are you kidding me right now?" Charlene said.

"Junior?" he asked.

"I'll have a dry martini."

"Wiseass," Jimmy replied. He rifled around in the refrigerator for a second, then said, "Hey! What happened to all the *gabagool?*"

"What are you talking about?" she said from the entryway. "We had three bags of it."

"Yeah, well, not no more. Somebody's been eating my *gabagool.*"

Charlene stepped into the kitchen. "Who would eat your *gabagool?* It's too spicy."

"I don't know, but somebody did. There's a couple slices missin'."

"What are you, counting slices now?"

"I know when food is missin', believe me."

"Well, you're the only one who eats that hot stuff. My sweet *gabagool* is right here in this...hey! Somebody's been eating my *gabagool.*"

"What are you, countin' slices?" he echoed.

"Yes," she answered.

Just then, Junior ran into the kitchen to see what all the fuss was about.

31

"What's wrong?" he asked.

"Somebody's been eating *my gabagool*," said Dad.

"Somebody's been eating *my gabagool*," said Mom.

Junior looked in the fridge, then on the counter, where his empty bag lay.

"Somebody's been eating my *gabagool*," he said. "And they ate it all up!"

"I don't like what's goin' on here," said Jim Senior.

"Hold that thought," Charlene said. "I gotta pee."

A few seconds went by, and then, "Ahhhhh!"

Dad and Junior rushed into the bathroom. "What is it?" Dad asked.

"Somebody's been messing with my hair gel!" she yelled.

"What the?" said Dad. "Somebody's been messing with *my* hair gel."

"Somebody's been messing with *my* hair gel," said Junior, "and spilled it all over the place."

"I don't like what's goin' on here," repeated Jim Senior. "I got a baaaad feelin'."

"Go check the rest of the house," Charlene told Jim.

"Wait here," he said to his wife and son, and went into the living room.

"Woah. Woah. Woah," he said. "Somebody's been sittin' in my chair."

"What are you talking about?" asked Charlene. "Nobody in their right mind would, oh no. Look at that. It's all reclined. And what the hell happened to Jimmy's bean bag chair?"

"What about my bean bag chair?" Junior asked as he entered the room, and instantly he started to cry. "Somebody broke my bean bag chair!" he wailed.

"I don't like what's goin' on here," said Jim Senior for the third time.

A smack landed across his face. "Hey!" he said. "What's your problem, Charl?"

"Somebody is laying on my couch," she said. "Who's the bimbo?" She pointed to the blond girl, still passed out.

"How the hell should I know?" he said in defense.

"Caught you red-handed," she said.

"Yeah," said Jim. "Caught you red...hey, wait. You talkin' to me?"

"Yes, I'm talking to you. I told you if I ever caught you with a *goomah*, we were through. And now, here she is, in our own house? And she can't be older than sixteen. Disgusting."

"You fuckin' kidding me right now?" he asked. "Junior, cover your ears. You think I'm fuckin' around with *this?*" He gestured at the sleeping girl.

"Oh, come on," Charlene said. "I know all about you men and what you get up to. My dad having a mistress tore apart my family. Don't give me that shit. You're all the same."

He cradled Charlene's face in his hands, slightly forceful, but not enough to hurt. "Charl, I ain't like the other guys. I ain't sleepin' with no woman behind your back. And if I was, do you think I'd invite him here, of all places?"

"Invite *him* here?" she echoed.

"Invite who here?" he asked.

"You just said invite him here," she said.

"Not sure who you're talkin' about. Invite who here? You know nobody's invited here unless they're invited."

"Then who is this?" she asked.

"That's just what I intend to find out. Junior, go to your room."

"But dad..."

"Don't but dad nothin'. Go to your room. Now."

He sighed and stomped up the stairs, slamming his door.

Jim took a seat on the couch beside the girl.

"Hey. Hey, Blondie, wake up."

She stirred, but not enough to awaken.

Jim hit her open-handed across the face.

"Ow! What the..."

"Jim, there's no need of that," Charlene said.

Ignoring his wife, he said, "Good mornin', sleepy head."

"Wha...? Where am I?"

"You're in the wrong fuckin' house, that's where you are." He breathed heavily through his nose, steam coming out of his nostrils. Her dazed look turned to one of fear. It was obvious she hadn't expected to have fallen asleep, and it was also obvious she hadn't expected to get caught.

"Wrong house!" she said. "That's it! Oh, man. Sorry, I thought this was my house. They look identical, you know. Except you don't live in my house, so this must not be my house. Yes, that's it. Common mistake. Well, I'm sorry to disturb you lovely folks. I'll just be on my way. Can you point me the way to Cavendish?"

"Wrong house, huh?" Jim said. "Well, sure. Of course. Happens all the time." He smiled. "Cavendish is about three miles that way." He pointed his finger.

"Ah, well thank you very much. Sorry for the inconvenience."

His smile became more sinister. "No problem, really. I guess you'll be on your way, then?"

"Yes. Let me just grab my...Where are my shoes? I know I put them somewhere."

He pointed by the door.

"Ah, yes well, again, sorry for all the trouble. Won't happen again, I promise."

As she opened the door to leave, she saw two police cruisers pulling into Jimmy's driveway. Officer Roberts got out of his vehicle and shot Jimmy a friendly wave, and Jimmy responded with the same gesture.

She turned to him, angrily. "You called the cops on me? What the fuck? Why would you do that? I told you it was a mistake."

"Oh really?" he said. "Do you make it a habit of breakin' your own window?" he gestured to the broken glass.

"What seems to be the trouble, Jimmy?" officer Roberts asked.

"Seems we have ourselves a little intruder," he answered.

"Is that right?" Roberts asked.

"Little bitch broke my window and ate my

gabagool."

"She ate your *gabagool?*"

"Yep. You know the rule: Never touch another man's meat." The irony was not lost on him.

"Are you the person who's been breaking into homes all throughout the tri-county area?"

"I thought they were mine," she responded.

"Come with me, missy. We're going downtown."

She glared at Jimmy. "I can't believe you called the cops."

"Believe me, honey," he said, "it beats the alternative."

Roberts laughed. "Sure does," he said, "It sure does."

He waved a childish wave to the blond girl as Officer Roberts pushed her down in the back seat of the cruiser.

"Bye-bye!" he shouted. "Don't be a stranger!"

She shot a finger out the rear window at him. A very bold gesture, but she had nothing to lose at this point.

6. Porridge

Blondie had been lucky most of her life. This was her first run-in with the law, and definitely her first time in jail. She hadn't even had any idea what the inside of one looked like until now. She needed to get out of here as quickly as possible, maybe even quicker than that.

Officer Roberts came around with a tray of food. "How ya doin', rich girl? Not used to this, are ya? I brought you some food."

He set the tray on the floor and slid it underneath the bars of her cell.

The officer looked at the steaming bowl of slop, and then at her, in much anticipation. Like he expected her to eat this.

"What is this?" she asked.

"Cream of Wheat," he answered.

"You mean *porridge?*"

"I guess so. Not a fan, huh?"

"Not really. Reminds me of a time I'd rather not think about."

"Well, you need to get used to it if you're going to live a life of crime. Your diet will consist of nothing but porridge and bologna sandwiches. And every Wednesday night is lobster mac n' cheese."

"Fancy," she said.

"Not really," he said, guiltily. "It comes in frozen."

"Well, I will not have time to get used to it. I'm getting out of here as soon as they set bail."

"Good for you," he said. "You know, today could have gone terrible for you. I've seen some things that have happened to those who ended up on the bad side of Jimmy DiFrenzo. And it ain't pretty, let me tell you. Why, I could tell you tales that would make your skin crawl."

"Ooh! Do tell!" she begged.

"You know, I really shouldn't. He's never been convicted of anything, so I probably should just leave it alone. But, since you asked so nicely, I guess it wouldn't hurt to tell you a few things. Remember that movie *8 Heads in a Duffel Bag*?"

"Yeah."

"Well, how about nine heads in a duffel

bag?"

"So?"

"So? It was one more head than the movie. Scary, huh?"

"That's nothing."

"Remember the movie *A Series of Unfortunate Events*?"

"Yeah."

"Well I knew a guy that after he double-crossed ole Jimmy, he was met with a series of even worse unfortunate events."

"And...?"

"And what?"

"What were they?"

"They were even worse unfortunate events. You know, like, *really bad.*"

Blondie yawned.

"Okay, okay, here's one. You know that movie *Pulp Fiction*?"

"Yeah, yeah?" she said excitedly.

"Well, sometimes people double-crossed Jimmy. And now they are bloody pulps. And they wished it was fiction."

"All you're doing is taking movie titles and twisting them up all silly. Can you give me some real dirt on the guy?"

"Okay, last one. You know the movie *Fargo*, right?"

"Yes, I know the movie *Fargo*."

"Well, one time someone double-crossed Jimmy, they had to move to Fargo to hide from him."

"And? Did he find the guy and separate his body parts? Did he toss him over a bridge with cement shoes? Did he give him to a guy in a Skyhawk who tossed his body into the frigid Arctic Ocean, where he soon froze into a block of ice?"

"Nope. Never found the guy."

"Has anyone ever told you that your stories are like, really boring?"

"Whatever. Eat your porridge. It ain't getting any tastier just sitting there."

She didn't have to spend the night there; however, she must have been dead tired, because before she knew it, she was sound asleep. She awoke in the morning refreshed. That night she spent in the cell was the best sleep she'd had in a long time. Anyway, it was time to go pay bail and get the hell out of there.

Officer Roberts opened the cell door.

"Where do I go to pay?" she asked.

"Right up at the window in the lobby," he said.

"Cool. Hey, thanks for all the laughs."

"Keep it moving." He gave her a fatherly look. "And I don't wanna see you back here, understand?"

"Whatever, After-School Special. It's been real."

She got up to the window.

"Can I help you?" the old gentleman behind the glass asked. He must have been a hundred and six years old if he was a day.

"Yeah, I'm here to pay my bail."

"Name?"

"Marguerite Bonaventure."

"Bonaventure...Bonaventure... let's see." He put on his reading glasses and perused through the list.

"Let me see," he repeated.

"Come on, pops. There ain't nobody else here. The list can't be too long."

"Let's see, Bradley, nope, Bauer, nope. Bonneville, hey you sure it's not Bonneville?"

"What's the bail for Bonneville?"

"Ten thousand."

"Nope. Bonaventure. You know, as in not Bonneville."

"Ah. Here it is. Bonaventure. First name?"

"How many Bonaventures are on that list? I just told you. Marguerite."

"Ah yes, Marguerite Bonaventure. Let's see. Um. Let's see here. Oh yes, here it is, Marguerite Bonaventure."

"Jesus Christ, can you speed it up a little?"

"Ah yes, Marguerite Bonaventure. Let me see here. Oh, um... yes, that's it. That'll be forty-eight dollars and uh, let's see... sixty-three cents.

"Okay, well you have my purse, so..."

"Your purse?"

"Yeah, you know, the thing ladies carry around to keep their money in?"

"Ah yes, your purse. Hmm, okay. Purses, now lemme see, where do we keep the purses?"

"You're kidding me."

"Ah, here they are. Now, what does your purse look like?"

"It's Vera Bradley."

"I thought you said you weren't Bradley. You said you was Bonaventure."

"No, the purse is... never mind. Just show me what you have, and I'll pick it out."

"Well, we only have the one here. Is this it?" he pulled her purse off the holding shelf.

"Yeah, that's it," she said in a get-me-the-hell-out-of-here tone. "If that was the only one, why... ah, forget it. Just hand it over."

"Okay, here ya go, sweetie."

She opened her wallet and pulled out her credit card. "Here."

"Oh, no. We only take cash here."

"You gotta be shitting me," she said.

"Sorry. That's the law. No credit cards for bail."

"Well. Here, then." She handed him two twenties and a ten. Good thing she kept cash on her at all times.

"Fifty dollars? I'm afraid I don't have change."

"You don't have change? You're a cashier, for Chrissakesssss."

"They don't give me change."

"Why such a strange amount set for bail, if you don't have change?"

"It's set by an algorithm I can't fathom," he answered.

"Fine, then. Keep the change."

"Oh, no, I can't do that. Exact change only. That's the law."

"Nowadays it's pure luck anyone would have cash on them at all, never mind exact change. Come on, can't you let me slide this once?"

"Afraid not," the old guy answered.

"There's nothing I can do to get out of here

today?"

"Call your folks," he said.

"Can't do that. My mom knows nothing about this."

"Call a friend."

"Don't have those."

"Call an aunt or uncle."

"They'd just tell my mom."

"Show me your boobies."

"I don't think... Wait, what?"

"Show me your boobies and I'll forget you don't have exact change." A line of drool exited his gaping maw and dropped onto the floor with a sickening *thud*.

"Fine," she said, and raised up her shirt for him as though she'd done it for hundreds of old men in her lifetime. She had, actually, but that's a separate story.

The old man's wig flipped off his skull, and his glass eye popped out and rolled onto the counter and onto the floor, where it ended up swimming in his saliva pool, calling for help.

"Hot-diggity-dog!" he shouted, hitting the button that unlocked the door that would release her back into the wild.

It sure was nice to feel the sunshine on her face again. Now, to get her revenge on DiFrenzo.

7. It's Good for Stains, Though.

What do you got for me, Lou?"

Lou hands over the envelope. Jimmy feels it in his hand briefly. "Little light," he says.

"Yeah, I know. I'll get you next week."

"Lou, you been sayin' that every week. When you gonna come through?"

"Next week, I swear."

Jimmy nods. Lou knows that nod. "I was being generous. It's *a lot* light."

There were eight people in the room, but there was the sound of zero. You could hear the proverbial pin drop.

"Look, I know this job ain't for everyone. And if you can't hack it, then maybe you need to find a different line of work."

"Look, Jimmy, I..."

"Don't I treat you good?"

"Sure?"

"Benefits not good enough for you? Health insurance and the like?"

"No, the benefits are fine, Jimmy, I…"

"Need another week's vacation?"

Lou knew that sometimes "vacation" didn't mean *vacation*. They all knew that. Everyone in the room was silently praying to the Blessed Virgin that Lou would make it till next week. All except Bobby. He had bet against Lou making it another week, and he had a lot of money riding on it.

"Yeah, boss. Maybe he needs another vacation," Bobby said, getting the look of death from Lou.

"Yeah," said Jimmy. "Maybe he does."

Lou gulped a loud, cartoon-ish gulp, heard by those in the room, everyone out in the bar, and even out on the dance floor of Stella.

Jimmy reached into the inside pocket of his sport coat as Lou braced himself for the inevitable. He slowly pulled his hand out from his pocket, revealing an envelope of his own. "Here," he said, handing the envelope to Lou.

"What's this?" Lou asked.

"Two tickets to Cancun. Take your wife Victoria and get away for a while. I was gonna take Charl, but you seem to need it more than

I do."

"Gee, I don't know what to say. Thanks, boss."

"Forget about it. Go. Get away. Clear your head. When you come back, I need you back in the game a hundred percent. *Capisce*?"

"Sure thing, Jimmy. You can count on me."

"Good. Now get outta here, you rapscallion."

"You bet! I'll pack tonight!"

"Now, Bobby. You had a lot to say earlier. Where's your envelope?"

"Here it is, boss," he said, and handed his own envelope over.

Jimmy weighed this one in his hand. "Hmm. This one's even lighter. What's with youse guys?"

"It's all there, boss. Count it."

"Don't tell me what to do!" he shouted. "Think I'll count it." He opened the envelope and dumped out the contents. Inside were a dozen handwritten checks.

"The fuck is this? Checks?"

"Yeah."

"Since when do we take checks, boss?" asked Joe

"I got this, Joe," said Jimmy. "Since when do we take checks, Bobby?"

"Well, see, I was thinkin',"

"Oh, this oughtta be a good one. Yeah? You were thinkin'?"

"Yeah, see, walkin' around with big wads of cash? Very dangerous. I could get robbed and whatnot. So I axed my customers to pay me by check. See, that way, I don't get robbed or nothin'."

Jimmy finished counting the amounts on the checks. "All here," he said.

"See? I told ya. I wasn't gonna stiff you or nothin'. Now, where's my vacation?"

"Oh, yours is coming. Joe, take this guy for a walk. Explain to him about checks and whatnot."

Joe led Bobby out of the room and up the elevator ten stories, the top floor of the building. As they walked down the corridor and toward the door that went to the roof, Joe talked about the magic of checks.

"See, Bobby, every week you come in here light, right?"

"Yeah, I guess I do," he said, embarrassed.

"It's not a big deal. People come in light all the time. It happens. We can let these accounts float for a week or so. Business has its ups and downs week to week; we get that. They just pay us a little extra the following week. It's how it's done. We make more money in the long run that way. Now, here you come with a handful of checks. Every cent paid. See the issue?"

"Nah. I don't see no issue."

"See, there's a reason we're a cash only business. Why do you think that is?"

"I don't know. Personally, I think we're doing it wrong."

"Okay, now here's the way I see the issue, the two main problems we face with checks. One, they're traceable. Now, if you had half a brain in your head, you would get why that ain't a good thing. Not least of which is taxes, and also the certain legalities, or lack thereof, of the business we're in."

He put his arm around Bobby's shoulder, leading him to the edge of the roof. Bobby was sweating profusely.

"You know another thing about checks, Bob?"

Tears sprang from Bobby's eyes as he shook his head vigorously.

"Come on, Bobby. Dry your eyes. Have some respect. I asked you a question. Do you know another thing about checks?"

"N-n-no," Bobby stammered.

"They bounce," Joe said, as he pushed him

off the edge.

Joe strolled back into the office, whistling a tune.

"Ay! How'd you make out? He understand our check policy now?"

"Oh yes. He won't be making that mistake no more."

Dollars flew in all directions, as those betting that Bobby wouldn't last through the week won their bets.

"You know, it really ain't appropriate, you guys makin' money off betting on the way I run my practice. What's this?" he asked, pointing to the pile of money in front of him.

"You won the bet too, Jimmy," Joe said.

"Ha! Well I'll be. Who wants some drinks? On me."

All raised their hands.

"Shirley Temple for you, Wagon Boy?" Jimmy asked Michael Imperioli, who was two years clean and sober.

"Yeah, the usual."

"You know, I'm awful proud of you, Wagon Boy," Jimmy said. "But if you're not gonna drink, at least order something a little more manly, like a club soda."

"But club soda's fucking disgusting," Michael Imperioli said.

And he was right; club soda was fucking disgusting.

"Yo, Tammy. The usual round for the usual dummies. 'Cept you can hold off on Bobby's drink. I don't think he'll be needing it."

Tammy stopped wiping a glass with her bar rag and chuckled. "Is that him I just heard hit the pavement out there?"

"Yeah. Dunno what happened. One minute he went out on the roof for a smoke, and the next... I told him smokin' would kill him one day. Remind me tomorrow to have someone put guardrails up there. This can't happen again."

Tammy laughed again. "Sure thing, Jimmy."

"How you doin' honey?" Jimmy asked the girl sitting at the bar nursing a drink of her own. "You okay?"

"Yep. Just finishing up here." The girl slammed down the rest of her beverage and got up off her stool. She turned to face him. "You know, you have a very nice establishment."

He recognized that face. "Blondie?"

She put on her coat and walked toward the door with a friendly wave. "Think I just found my new watering hole," she shouted to a flabbergasted Jimmy as she went out.

8. Your Ma Made Lasagna

Hey Charl," he said when he strolled through the door. She gave him a kiss, and he kissed her back with much gusto.

"Mmm. Tough day at the office?" she asked.

"How'd you know?"

"You always kiss me like that when you've had a rough day."

"I do? Ha. I never noticed. I needed to feel your lips against mine for a while."

"Awww."

All that was wrong with the world just melted away every time he kissed her. She was his everything. It was a shame he slept around on her with Joe, but Joe had one thing she didn't have. A tattoo. Ha. Just kidding. I meant cock.

"Where's our child?" he asked.

"He's in his room."

"What's he doin' there?"

"No idea. Now that I think about it, I haven't seen him all day. I was wondering why it was so peaceful here."

Knock knock.

"Come in."

Jimmy opened the door to find Junior lying in bed, reading a book. So studious!

"Hey, Champ."

"Hi Dad."

"Whatcha doin' in here?"

"You told me to go here."

"I did?"

"Remember? When the girl was here?"

"That was yesterday," said Jimmy. "You haven't come out since?"

"Nobody told me I could."

"For the life of me, I don't understand how you get straight A's."

"*Used* to get straight A's. I don't know how I'm gonna do at St. Mark's."

"You'll do fine, kid. Your dad went to St. Mark's, and look how he turned out."

A tear came to Junior's eye.

"Hey, now. I find that kind of insultin'."

"Sorry, Dad. Nothing against you. I just, I don't know. I guess I'm excited to go, but a little nervous too. What if I don't make any friends?"

"You didn't have friends at your old school," answered Jimmy.

A few more tears rolled down Junior's cheeks.

"Aw, come on. I didn't mean that. Listen, you know half the kids going there. You'll be fine."

"You really think so?"

"I do," said Jimmy, as he picked at his teeth with his heavily ringed pinky finger.

"Something in your teeth?"

"Yeah. Think it's *gabagool* from yesterday."

Junior broke into a full-on sob

"Now what's the matter?" his dad said.

"Somebody ate all my *gabagool*."

"You can have some of mine."

"It's too spicy!" he wailed.

"For the love of... Come eat. Your ma made lasagna. You must be starvin'."

"I haven't eaten anything all day," said Junior.

"Why not?"

"Nobody told me I could."

"Hold on a second," Jimmy said, and pulled out the back of his boy's pants..

"What are you doing?"

"Makin' sure you're wipin' your ass.

Nobody told you to do that either."

They went down the stairs together.

"Dad?"

"Yeah?"

"Do you *really* think I'll like St. Mark's?"

"I do. I really do. Now, let's eat," he said, then mumbled, "Your dad wants to go to the titty bar."

"What's *that*?" Junior asked.

"I said your ma's lasagna is the best by far."

"Sure is," Junior said.

9. The Blue Iguana

The Blue Iguana wasn't the best strip club in the city, and it wasn't the worst. It was a very medium-type place. It had re-opened just a little over a year ago, after the place was burned to the ground by a Molotov cocktail a disgruntled employee threw through a window. The tits were good, and on nights like tonight they were just plain weird, but the food was pretty damn fantastic for pub food. And it was never really busy like the places further downtown, so Jimmy could go and relax and get his mind off of things. Tonight was a typical night at the club, except it was the first Friday of the month. First Fridays were called "Freaky Fridays" at the Iguana, and they were anything but typical, so this, being a first Friday, was also a Freaky Friday, and it wasn't really typical at all.

"...And next on the stage, the tattooed

beauty, Alexis," the dude with the microphone said from a table at the edge of the room.

Alexis was an interesting case. She had no noticeable tattoos, but there were two very large tats covering her breasts. There was no detail, and they were the color of her own skin, and the artist had somehow created the illusion that she had no breasts. Once you got within reach (NOT THAT YOU COULD TOUCH), however, it was obvious her protuberances were quite large indeed. It was wild.

"Hey yo, more peanuts over here!" came a shout from a few tables over.

"I just gave you peanuts!" came the annoying high-pitched voice of the waitress.

"Then somebody's been eating my peanuts!"

"...Thank you Alexis, and next to the stage, the...um...interesting... Donna!"

Donna came to the stage, hauling her tits around like two wet mules; dragging on the ground, literally. And by literally, I don't mean figuratively. Her specialty was tying her bazoombas in a knot. And she didn't just have one knot in her repertoire, either. She could do knots that would make a boy scout blush. I'm talking double sheet bend, trucker's hitch, clove hitch, double fisherman's knot, timber hitch, the list went on and on. By the tenth knot, Jimmy had tired of the show. With tits that long, there were hundreds of other things she could do with them, but no, just knots.

"Could I please get more peanuts?" Came a more polite request for nuts.

"You too?" said the waitress. "I just filled your bowl."

"Somebody's been eating *my* peanuts."

"Hey, mine too!" shouted someone else. "And they ate 'em all up!"

Hmm. There was something about this situation that seemed familiar to Jimmy, and it wasn't old Knotty Tits up on stage. It was food related. Perhaps the person who was stealing everyone's peanuts was the same one who stole the gabagool. Or maybe there was an elephant in the room.

A large trunk slithered its way over his shoulder, down his chest, and over to his table grabbing a peanut. Awww. There was an elephant in the room. Every Freaky Friday there was a circus animal there, to add to the overall theme. Jimmy wasn't sure how Myron, the owner of the bar, could afford such exotic animals. He was contemplating this when a shout came from backstage. "Hey, watch it! Hey Charlie, somebody just touched my tits!"

"Watch the tit touching, there," the man with the microphone said.

"Shoo, elephant. Go on, git!" The elephant, determined to eat the peanuts, could not be distracted. Still, there's no way she could have eaten as many peanuts as the customers claimed. Somebody else must have been eating the...

"Somebody just touched my tits, too," another voice came from back stage.

"Sir and/or madam, I will ask you one more time nicely to...hey, somebody's touching my tits, too. And here she comes, onstage now, the gorgeous, can't-believe-she's-legal blond from parts unknown, Marguerite!

There she was, walking onto the stage. That little bitch. Jimmy looked at her body as she started taking off articles of clothing, her eyes locked on him the entire time. There was nothing unusual or freaky about her, so he wasn't sure what she was doing here on this night of all nights, but...Woah. Okay, *that* was freaky. Jimmy hadn't seen anyone do that before. He looked away in embarrassment, as he knew damn well she was underage.

When her act finished, she clumsily gathered up the dollar bills that the customers had thrown onto the stage, walked off, and took a seat at Jimmy's table.

"Hey," she said.

"Hey," he said. "Look, if you're gonna sit here, put some clothes on or somethin'."

She gave a fake pout. "What's the matter? Don't like what you see?"

"Oh, for the love of…How'd you even get in here? Aren't you like, a teenager or somethin'?"

"Seventeen."

"Don't you have to be twenty-one in this state?"

She laughed. "You think anyone gives a shit?"

"Probably not. So anyways, what do you want from me?"

"I want to be friends."

"Ha!"

"What's so funny?" she asked.

"You wanna be friends, huh?"

"Yeah. Friends."

"We can't be friends. We'll never be friends."

"Why not?"

"Do you even know who I am?" he asked.

Yes, I know who you are. Everyone knows who you are."

"Then I ask again, what do you want from

me?"

"Why did you call the cops on me?"

He laughed. "Is that it? You wanna know why I called the cops? You broke into my house!"

"So? I stole nothing from you. Except a few beers and some salami."

"*Gabagool.*"

"Whatever."

"Anyway, it's not about the stealin'. You can't go around breakin' into houses."

"Why not?" she asked.

He couldn't believe he was sitting here having this conversation with a naked teenager. "Are you serious right now?"

"Yes. Why can't I do whatever I want? *You* can."

"I don't do whatever I want. In life, there are rules we all have to follow. If you don't follow them, then you gotta learn from your mistakes. That's why I called the cops."

"Oh, like you ever learn from your mistakes?"

"You fuckin' kidding me?" He lifted the front of his shirt up so she could see the nasty scar he had on his stomach. "See that? That's a lesson learnt. See those?" He gestured at the scars across all the crooked fingers on his left hand. "I was a lefty before this. Had to have them all sewn back on after some mook cut them off. I learnt a lesson there, too. Can't even bend these two fingers. See that?"

"Wow, you must have done something horrible to warrant that."

"Not *that* horrible. That mook crossed the line on that one. And so, he learnt his own lesson shortly thereafter."

"Tell me more about that."

"Well see, what happened was... heyyy, wait a minute. You're not gonna get me to talk just 'cause I had a few bourbons. I'm a pro at keepin' my mouth shut.

"And so you killed him, right? No big deal, right? Did it make you feel better?"

"Not really. That's not what it's about. And anyway," he winked, "I didn't kill nobody."

She wondered if a double negative could legally be considered a confession.

"Anyway, you see what I'm gettin' at, right? And jail? You're all bent out of shape over spending one night in jail? You think I ain't been to jail? Ha!"

"And you're still doing what you've always done."

"Yes, but I learnt from it. I'm smarter now. I don't fall asleep on people's couches."

"Good to know. I hear your kid got kicked out of school. Following in his old dad's footsteps?"

"How did you hear that?"

"Never mind how. I know more about you than you think."

"For your information, he wasn't kicked out. We pulled him out. He's goin' to St. Mark's."

"Oh, well isn't that cute? He can hang out with all the other mob kids. What he hasn't already learned from you he can learn from them."

"Keep your voice down."

"Or what?!" she shouted.

"For the third time," said Jimmy, "what do you want from me? You here to blackmail me? Is that it?"

"Hmm, I never thought of that," Blondie said. "You got something I can use?"

"Clean as a whistle."

"Hahahaha. That's a riot." She headed out the door, then turned and shouted to him. This was her signature move. "Catch you on the flip!" she said, and left.

He laughed. She forgot her clothes. Something was not right with this chick. As of now, she was just a kid with maybe a screw or two loose. She was annoying him, but it was nothing to have her whacked over. He needed to be careful of her, though. She reeked of trouble.

10. Meatballs

He checked his watch. Ten o'clock. The night was still young and he didn't feel tired. He should probably go to Stella and get some work done. For some unknown reason, he felt frisky. It wasn't the knot girl, or vanishing tit girl. It wasn't the elephant, and it wasn't Blondie. It was most likely the bourbon. Chances are Charlene was already in bed, curled up with a good book, or maybe even sound asleep. Either way, he wasn't getting any from her tonight. He dialed his phone.

"Hello?"

"Hey, Joe. What's happenin'?"

"Ah, nothin'. At my ma's house. She thought she heard a noise. Come to find out it was just my father fallin' down the steps again."

"Again? What is that, the third time this year?"

"Third time this *month*. I think she pushes him and neither one remembers 'cause they're both so fuckin' senile. Anyway, I was just about to head home. What's up?"

"I was just at Freaky Friday at the Iguana."

"I see. And now you wanna fuck, right?"

"Shh. Not so loud! Your parents!"

"My parents? They are so out of it they don't know what the fuck is going on. Listen to this... Hey ma! I'm gonna go fuck Jimmy in the ass at the club. You wanna join?"

In the background, he heard Joe's mother say: "Take him some meatballs!"

"See what I mean, Jimmy? Anyway, you want some meatballs?"

"I just ate so much at the Iguana, I don't think I can eat one more bite." After a second's pause, he said, "Bring 'em anyway; you never know."

"Ten-four," Joe said.

"Tin foil?" Jimmy heard Joe's dad shout. "Who's the tin foil man?"

"See you in thirty," Joe said.

Jimmy sat behind his desk in the office, trying to get more paperwork done. Usually a few drinks helped him through the monotony of this process, but tonight he had too many and could not concentrate. He looked at his watch again. Joe wasn't late yet, but Jimmy was getting anxious about it anyway. He went down to the bar and got another bourbon to help calm his nerves and settle his sausage a little.

A knock-knock sounded at the door, followed by the door opening, followed by a verbal "knock-knock." It was Joe, carrying a tray of meatballs."Jesus, Joe, you ain't gotta knock. Also, you ain't gotta say *knock knock.* Makes you sound like a fag."

"Ha. Coming from the man who sucks the best dick this side of the Mason-Dixon."

"Hey, watch it. Next time I just might bite it off."

"Ooh, promises promises," Joe said in a femmey voice.

"All right, quit talkin' in a femmey voice. And lock the door, will ya?"

He locked the door, turned around, and dropped his drawers.

"Nothin' like gettin' down to business, hey, Joe?"

"I gotta be home by midnight or the wife gets pissy," Joe said.

"Who's runnin' the show at your house, anyway?"

"Heh heh. You know the answer to that one. I'm just happy she hasn't noticed me coming home smelling like your cock."

"Okay, less talkin' and more fuckin'."

And they did. For ten solid minutes, they had some nasty man-on-bear action.

"Ah, ah, ah, AAAAHHH MEATBALLS!" Jimmy shouted as he came.

"Shh, that's wicked loud."

"Sorry," said Jimmy. "These are some superb meatballs!" he yelled as a cover, just in case someone else heard him coming. Also, they *were* good meatballs, he was thinking as he ate a couple. Not as good as Charlene's, but damn good

"So," Joe said as he zipped up, "catch me up on all that's been goin' on. What's the deal with Blondie?"

He had told Joe a little of the Blondie story previously, but now he told him everything: The popping up in random places, the stripping, the feeling that she was up to something.

"Maybe she *is* up to somethin'," Joe suggested, as he munched on a meatball.

"Yeah, but what?"

"Dunno. Maybe she's tryin' to blackmail you or somethin'."

"She said she just wanted to be friends. That was all. Besides, she ain't got nothin' on me to blackmail me with."

Joe roared, hearty and strong.

"What?" Jimmy asked.

"Are you nuts? Did you forget who you were for a second? Did you fall down a flight of stairs and bump your head? You're as bad as my mom and dad, for Christ sakes. Someone could pull up a whole bunch of things on you if they dug hard enough."

"Get real," he said as he munched. "She ain't that bright," Jimmy said. "Plus, she said she don't want nothin' from me. She's got money, and I don't know what else she'd want."

"Well, it's gotta be somethin'. Believe me, with females, it's always somethin'."

And Joe was right. It was something. And there, in the supply closet, between the reams of paper and boxes of staples, there was a ship in a bottle that Jimmy had built. And there, in that ship in a bottle, was a small camera that a blond girl had planted in there when no one was looking.

And there, at home in her bedroom, sitting on her computer, a mischievous grin on her face, Blondie was watching the whole thing.

11. Gabagool

Got you, you sonofabitch," she said.

She hit stop, saved the video as a file, and made a copy on a thumb drive. She had him right where she wanted him, now. She could do anything, anything, with the file. Either way she used it, it would completely ruin him.

The question was, what should she do with it? Should she leave it for Jimmy's wife to see? Surely that would be the end of their relationship. His family, the most important thing in life to him, destroyed, in a matter of minutes. She could just imagine the look on his wife's face as she watched him plowing his best friend from behind. Her husband. A, what did they call it? *Fanook*? Her husband, a *fanook*. What a riot! She'd take the boy and leave. Or better yet, she'd kick him out of his own house and take him for everything he had. But was that the worst thing that could happen to him? It was terrible, yes, but she didn't think it was the worst thing. His wife may divorce him, but she may also try to keep it a secret, and just make up some other story about why she kicked him out. For one, she could be nice and not want to see Jimmy humiliated. And her husband fooling around on her with another man? She'd also feel humiliated, and it would scar her son for life. Charlene wouldn't want that.

She could send it to Charlene's dad, the real head of the family. Jimmy would lose his job for sure. And in the mafia, there was only one way to lose your job. You either fled and ended up in witness protection, or you stopped breathing. She knew the old man wouldn't give Jimmy a chance to run, so that left the other option. For sure he'd cease to exist, but again, she didn't think that was the worst thing. Most likely, the old man would kill him mercifully and blame it on a rival. She knew how the mob worked. Jimmy had done a lot of good things for the Family. He had brought in a lot of wealth, and had helped moved up the Family's status. And one indiscretion, however large it may seem, would not outweigh all the good Jimmy had done so far. No, his death would be quick and painless. He needed to die, for sure, but before that happened, he needed to have his name shamed. He needed his world to come crashing down around him before someone offed him. And if it shamed Jimmy, it shamed the entire Family. Then his death wouldn't be so quick and painless. Bringing embarrassment to the Family was the worst thing that could happen. His father-in-law would share the shame, and he would have no choice but to set an example of Jimmy, just to save face. It would be incredible. They would shame him, then torture and kill Jimmy. This had to become a scandal. But how?

She needed to brainstorm. Perhaps a little weed would help her mind think more clearly. She fired up her volcano vaporizer, filled the plastic bag with weed vapor, and inhaled the whole thing in one in-breath. She'd never taken the whole bag in like that, and it instantly made her head dizzy. She lay down and closed her eyes.

She wasn't sure if what she saw was a dream or not, but she envisioned herself lost in the woods. She was tired, hungry, and thirsty, and was about to give up, when she saw a cabin in the distance and headed for it. Arriving at the door, she turned the knob. Hmmm...locked.

She took a rock and threw it through a window, then climbed inside. She was really in the mood for some capicola, but she could find no fridge. Instead, what she found were three bowls of what appeared to be porridge resting on the counter. This reminded her of her time in jail. She tried the first bowl, which was too hot. The next bowl was too cold and congealed, like wallpaper paste. Although she enjoyed a good wallpaper paste from time to time, this was worse. She moved onto the third bowl, which was exactly the right temp, which made little sense. It should have been the coldest of the three, as it was the smallest bowl and thus should have cooled the fastest. Regardless, she knew that's how the story went, so who was she to argue?

She was right in the middle of the most thermally pleasing of the three bowls of porridge (which, incidentally, still tasted like shit), when she heard keys rattling in the front door's lock. She quickly scanned the cabin for a place to hide, but it was very open concept, as most fabled cabins in the woods were. She felt doomed.

In barged a giant bear with gold chains and a nice suit. *Gabagool!* he shouted. The mother bear walked in behind him. *Gabagool!* she screamed. The baby bear was the last to enter, and when he saw her still eating his food, he shouted, *Gabagool! Haha!* His dad said, pointing at him. *Private school!*

Private school. That's it. Oh, thank you to the gods of weed, they gave her the answer she had been looking for. She knew just where to send the thumb drive. This was gonna be good.

12. St. Mark's

Sister Mary Josephine, St. Mark's resident professor of Calculus and New Testament studies, and the founder of Stigmata Awareness Month, went through the daily mail. Amongst all the propaganda from the Church of Scientology (who the hell added them to their mailing list, she'd never know) and Applebee's coupons, there was a small manila envelope. She opened it up, and a thumb drive fell out with a note: PLAY ME.

Fearing something Satanic lurked within, and therefore not wanting to touch it, she went to the office and knocked on Father Healy's door. I could do the cliché thing, and make a joke about how there was a boy with no trousers on in his office, but that would be crass, and frankly a joke that's been overkill for twenty years. Not only that, abuse in the Catholic church is a very serious issue.

Nothing to laugh or joke about. So I will only mention, in passing, that there was a boy there, with no trousers on in his office, rather than make the usual joke.

"Father Healy?"

"What is it, Sister?"

"We just received something in the mail that may or may not be very disturbing and I think you should take a look at it."

"I'll be right there. Hold that pose, Jeremy," he told the boy, and went into the hall, shutting the door behind him.

He looked at the pile of mail, and the thumb drive cast off to the side, along with the note.

"What do you think it is?" he asked.

"It's a thumb drive," Sister Mary Josephine said.

"No shit. I mean, what do you think is on it?"

"Beats me. It may be something Satanic."

"Or worse," he said. "It could be Scientologic."

She shuddered at that thought. "Come to think of it, there has been an unusual amount of Scientology propaganda in the mail. Who put us on all these mailing lists?"

"I don't understand. I tried to cancel the subscription, but then received a letter in the mail stating they would label me a Suppressive Person, forever considered an enemy of the Church, and then Kirstie Alley would stop my Jenny Craig subscription. And we can't have that."

"Come to think of it, you have slimmed down lately."

"Thank you. You know, Jeremy was just saying the same thing? Come on, let's see what's on this thing."

"Wait!" Sister Mary Josephine said in fear. "Don't pop it in just yet!"

"You know," Father Healy said, "Jeremy was just saying the same thing."

Sorry.

They put the thumb drive in the nearest computer and opened it. There was only one file in there, named JDF. Father Healy double-clicked on the file, and Windows Media Player opened up to play the filthiest video he'd ever seen. Well, it wasn't the *filthiest* video he'd ever seen, let's get real; not even close. However, it was the worst horror Sister Mary Josephine had ever witnessed, and she'd seen quite a few exorcisms and Leah Remini's documentary on Scientology.

"God," she blasphemed, "it's terrible. Turn it off, please!"

He was about to, but said, "Wait."

"For what?" she asked desperately.

"They sent us this for a reason. We need to watch the whole thing through." Plus, this was giving him a slight erection, which was more than he could say for Jeremy.

I said I'm sorry!

There was something about this video, other than the fact that it was turning him on. Specifically, something about the man in the back. He looked familiar to him.

"Sister, does the man standing up look at all familiar to you?"

"I can't see!" she said, as she had covered her own eyes.

Father Healy paused the video and covered up the bottom half of the screen with his hand. "Okay, now look."

"Oh my God."

"Sister! Language!"

"Sorry. I meant oh, *fuck*!"

"Who is that man?" Healy asked.

"That, sir, is Jimmy DiFrenzo."

"Oh, shit!"

"Double shit. You just enrolled his boy here."

"Oh no! Well, that was a mistake. For sure. We can't have that. We need to notify the family right away. His boy can't come here. Not after this."

"This is a big deal," Sister Mary Josephine said.

"This is a *gigantic* deal," Healy echoed.

Now, even though the Catholic church had put their foot down on priests and little boys, they had loosened their stance on homosexuality; especially since the election of the "cool pope". That little Jimmy DiFrenzo's father was gay had no bearing on his son going to school there, or rather, it wouldn't have any bearing, if Jimmy Senior was open about it.

Blackmailing the man was out of the question. There were countless examples throughout history of attempts to blackmail someone in the mob. None had good outcomes. He would have to go with the next best thing: Selling the story. Father Healy would expose this scandal for all it was worth, and would make sure he got every dime he could. It would mean lots of money for the church, after whatever he deemed fair to skim off the top for himself first.

"Call the papers, Sister," he said. "We're gonna be rich!"

13. Awfully Sorry

Charlene's cell phone rang.

"Hello?"

"Hi, Mrs. DiFrenzo, this is Father Healy from St. Mark's. How are you today?"

"Oh, hi, Father. Just fine, thank you. How are you?"

"I'm okay, thanks. I was wondering if you or your husband had some time tomorrow to meet for coffee, and discuss some things?"

"Gee, I wish we could, Father. But I have a lot going on this weekend, and my husband has his work, you know."

"His...work. Right."

"Is everything okay?" she asked. "Can we talk about it Monday when we come sign the paperwork?"

"Well, uh, that's what I wanted to talk to you about. I really didn't want to do this over the phone. After much review and deliberation, uh it seems we, uh, we can't accept Jimmy here, after all."

"WHAT?" she shouted.

"What's going on?" Jim Sr. called up from the basement when he heard her shout. He had been tinkering down there, fixing the auger in his snow blower. Sure, there were months to go before the snow fell, but, dear friends, if you get nothing else out of this book, heed these words: Test your snow blower before winter hits. You don't want to get stuck in a storm without a working snow blower.

"Father Healy said they can't take Jimmy," she yelled to him.

He raced up the stairs. "What are you talking about?"

"They can't take Jimmy," she said through her tears.

"Gimme that." He grabbed the phone out of her hand.

"Hi, Father? James DiFrenzo here."

"Hi, Mr. DiFrenzo."

"What's this about you can't take my son?"

"I'm very sorry," Father Healy said.

"Fuck!"

"Jim!" Charlene scolded.

"Sorry, Father," he said.

"It's all right. I know this probably comes as a shock to you. I just wanted to let you know as quickly as I could, before you pulled him out of public school."

"That's already done," Jimmy said.

"I'm sorry to hear that," Father Healy said. "I'm sure they'll take him back. They have to. It's a public school, after all."

"Why the change, suddenly?"

"I can't really disclose why at the moment."

"Bullshit!"

"Jim!" Charlene scolded again.

"No! I have a right to know. You can't just reject my son without lettin' me know why. What did he do?"

"It's nothing he did. Believe me. Like I said, for now I can't disclose the reason, but, please, believe me, you will know as soon as humanly possible. I just wanted to make sure Jimmy stayed in school so he won't fall behind. Good day, Mr. DiFrenzo."

The line went dead. Jimmy dialed the number that the call came from, but it went straight to voice mail.

"Son of a bitch," Jimmy said.

Charlene blew her nose into an old grocery receipt, as they were out of tissues. It never occurred to her that she could use toilet paper.

Grocery store receipts were not known for their absorbency, as they were not intended to be used to mop up messes on the kitchen counter or absorb mucus, so the snot made a white and yellow messy streak all over her mouth and cheeks.

"Oh, Jimmy. What did our boy do this time?"

"Our boy? Our boy did nothin'. Just a bunch of fucked-up politics, is all. They don't want to let us in because they know what I do for a living. You got a little somethin' there," Jimmy said, and he wiped Charlene's face with his handkerchief.

"Honey, that makes no sense. Half the children in there are just like our son. There has to be another reason."

Oh yeah, there was another reason, he just knew it. That blond-headed bitch was behind all this. He wasn't sure how, but one way or another he would figure the situation out.

Right on cue, his phone rang.

"Hello?" he answered.

"Hi Jimmy! It's me!"

That fucking she-devil had the nerve to call him. How did she get his number? *Nobody* outside of his family, and his other family, had his number. Also, what perfect timing. It's almost as though she knew that he had just been talking to the school. Did she have his house bugged? His phone tapped? What was her deal? She needed to go, there was no doubt in his mind. She *had* to, or she'd continue fucking with him forever. He wasn't sure why she had it in for him so badly; just because she spent a night in jail? Get over it. It wasn't a big deal, and he was planning on dropping the charges. She didn't know that, but still. She had it out for him, and it occurred to him that that meant the same as having it *in* for him. Same as calling *out* sick versus calling *in* sick. They mean the same thing too. It makes no sense to me, and it made no sense to him. His head was boiling. It had all been harmless up to this point, but now she had gone too far. Something she did had messed with his son's education. She needed to die.

"Oh, hi," he answered jovially. He couldn't let on that he was going to kill her, or that he suddenly learned that *in* and *out* could mean the same thing. Best to keep it casual.

"I gotta take this," he said to Charlene.

She nodded. She knew what that meant. Business call.

"What's going on?" she asked. Was that a giggle?

"Just got off the phone with St. Mark's. They can't take Jimmy."

"Oh. So sorry to hear that," she said. He knew fake sincerity when he heard it. It surrounded him all the time, from practically everyone he knew. Even Joe. But it was best to just play into her bullshit, for now.

"Hey, I was just thinkin' about you," he said.

"Oh, really?" said Blondie.

"Really. You know, I've been thinkin'. I'm gonna drop the breakin' and enterin' charges."

"Why?" she asked.

"What do you mean *why*? I thought you'd be happy about it."

"Oh, I am," she said. "I'm just wondering why the sudden change of heart."

"Remember that speech I gave last night, about how I learnt my lessons by going to jail?"

"Vividly."

"Yeah, well, it ain't true. I haven't learnt shit."

"No?"

"No. I just learnt how to be more crafty and not get caught. Didn't make me a more law-abiding citizen. In fact, just the opposite."

"I know. I mean, it's obvious."

"I guess I just wanted to teach you not to mess with me, is all."

"Duly noted."

"The more I thought about it, though, the more I realized, people don't respond to punishment as much as they do to kindness. And I know everyone thinks the contrary, but I have a good heart."

"Sure," she said.

"That's why I've decided to give you a college education. So you can make somethin' of yourself."

"Wait, what? Give me a college education? You're gonna teach me?"

"What? No. I'm gonna pay for your school. I wanna see you on the right track. Anywhere you wanna go, name it, and it's yours."

"Oh, Jimmy, I can't accept that. Besides, my mom can afford it."

"It ain't about affordin' it. You *can* accept it and you *will*. Case closed. One stipulation."

"What's that?"

"No more breaking into houses."

"Consider it done."

"Also, I ain't payin' for a liberal arts degree or women's studies. I don't wanna see you workin' at Dick's Sportin' Goods when you graduate. Anyways, what's up?"

"You know," she said, "I forgot why I called."

"That's okay. I'm glad you did. What are you doing tomorrow, around lunch time?" he asked coyly.

"Nothing that I know of," she answered, also coyly.

"How 'bout I take you out to lunch tomorrow, at Rossi's, my treat?" he asked. *And then I'll murder you,* he thought.

"Sounds great," she said. *And then I'll murder you,* she thought.

He looked down at his shirt and found a slice of bread left over from dinner stuck to it. Friggin' bread. Always landing butter-side down. He pulled it off like a soggy Band-Aid, dunked it in some sauce that had fallen on his lap, and stuffed it in his yapper. Mmmm, nothing like leftovers!

"Sho," he said through a mouthful of gluten, "She you tomarrah, eleven firty."

"Right on," she said, and hung up the phone. "You fat fucking pig," she added.

14. I Don't Know But I Don't Feel So Good

She sat on the edge of her bed, running her hands along the smooth surface of her Glock, not knowing how to feel. She should feel thrilled, instead she felt nervous. He deserved torture, like, a lot. But she didn't have it in her. A quick bullet to the head would have to suffice. She didn't know what she was doing, she had never even shot a gun before. Why in the hell did she think this would work? She would fail at this, just like she did at everything else.

Calm down, Marguerite, don't overthink it. Just go meet him tomorrow, and if the time seems right, if there's no one around, aim, click, boom. Simple. If not, try again when the scenario seems better. He has to be caught off-guard. And absolutely no witnesses, or you, my dear, are fucked.

She needed to stop worrying about it; right

now she should probably get some sleep. It was getting late, and she should be as well-rested as possible for the next day.

...Which came sooner than she wanted. She didn't get any sleep the night before. Her head was spinning like she had a hang over, but she had nothing alcoholic to drink the night before. This was just sheer exhaustion.

It was only eight in the morning. There was time to have two cups of coffee before she even tried to get ready. She opened the pantry door to get the coffee, and discovered there were no filters. "Ugh," she said in frustration. She tore a paper towel off the roll and attempted to fold it so it would fit in the basket. Try as she might, though, she couldn't get it into the shape she needed.

Come on, Blondie, you've done this before. You can make it work.

On the first attempt at folding, she made a swan. On the second attempt, a frog. On the third attempt, a bust of Beethoven. Somehow folding a square into a simple triangle was baffling her. Finally, she crumpled it into a ball, threw some coffee grounds on it, and turned it on. She'd let that brew while she took a shower.

The shower did nothing to wake her up.

And after chewing on three cups of coffee grounds, she was still just as tired. *Maybe another hour of sleep,* she thought, and headed back to bed to toss and turn for sixty minutes before giving up.

She felt worse. It felt like someone had beat her with a shoe. Maybe she was getting mono, or the flu, or something. Briefly, she contemplated calling Jimmy and telling him she couldn't make it. Briefly. Terrible idea. She had a feeling that he had a feeling that she was up to something. She couldn't quite put her finger on it, but there was something suspicious in the way he sounded on the phone. If she called him up and canceled, it might piss him off. It was best to play it cool and keep the lunch date.

She got up out of bed, struck by a wave of dizziness. She glanced at the clock. Quarter past ten. Time to get ready. One quick glance in the mirror told her she needed to put on a lot of makeup. There weren't just dark circles under her eyes, there were dark circles *all around* her eyes. It looked like she got in a bar fight with a Korean delivery boy.

Eleven o'clock. Time to head out. She picked her Glock off the bed, opened her desk drawer, placed it in gently, and closed it. Today was not the day for murder.

15. I Don't Know What You Mean, I Feel Great!

He sat on the edge of his bed, running his hands along the smooth surface of his Smith and Wesson Model 19. He was excited to get this over with. Blondie deserved torture. He wasn't sure he wanted to waste the time and effort it took to do that, though. He may just put a quick bullet in her head. Priority was getting rid of her. She needed to go. She wasn't a physical threat, but he had no clue what that unstable little bitch was capable of. She already got his boy kicked out of school before he even began, but how? Could it be that he was wrong? Maybe it had not been her. If only they'd told him over the phone what happened. Should he wait till he found out the reason? They told him he would know soon enough, but what if she pulled something else in the meantime? She was horrible, vindictive, and he needed to stop her. Now.

Just go meet her tomorrow, Jimmy, and if the time seems right, if there's no one around, aim, click, boom. Simple. If not, try again when the scenario seems better. Catch her off-guard. And with no witnesses.

Anyway, it was getting late and he needed to get his rest for tomorrow. "You coming to bed, Charl?" he yelled down the stairs.

"Be up in a bit," she yelled up.

And later on she would be. It wasn't often she went to bed after him, but when she did, she had the ability to slip in unnoticed, without waking him up. So he put the gun on the dresser. He didn't want to fall asleep with it in bed and have it accidentally shoot Charlene in the face.

He woke up feeling great. It was eight in the morning. Plenty of time to have a few cups of coffee before he needed to get his day rolling. He opened the pantry door. Which coffee should he start the day off with today? Ahh, yes. French roast. His favorite. But don't tell the other guys that. Real Italians drink espresso. He put the filter in the basket, put the grounds in the filter, hit ON, and it started its drip. He was falling right into stride today.

While that was going, it was time for his

shower. It sure felt nice. Today he even scrubbed behind his ears and in his belly button. Plus, he washed his feet, for the first time ever. I mean, who does that? Standing in the soapy water is usually enough, but not for Jimmy. Not today. He wanted to be extra clean for the special occasion.

He didn't think it was possible to feel any better, but dammit if the shower didn't make him even more happy and upbeat than he was when he first got up. "Plenty of sunshine headin' my way," he sang as he poured himself a cup of coffee in the nude.

"Hey dad," little Jimmy said, as he gazed at his dad's little jimmy.

"Zippity doo dah, zippity ay!" he continued to sing as he sipped his coffee and skipped merrily down the hall and back up the stairs.

"Mr. bluebird on my shoulder," Junior could hear all the way in the kitchen. He didn't know why his dad was in such a good mood, especially after the news he got last night.

Jimmy Senior was in a good mood, even after the news he got last night. He was always in high spirits when he would kill someone.

Now fully clothed, he stepped outside onto the porch to get the morning paper. The paperboy had thrown it high into the tree.

That was okay, though. Nothing could spoil his mood today. Until he got it down from the tree and looked at the front page. The headline read MOB BOSS OUT! Underneath it was his photo. He had never directly made the front page of the paper. Nothing good could come from this. And right next to his bulbous head, was Joe's head. Jimmy looked like he was shouting, and Joe looked like he was in agony. When he unfolded the paper to see the bottom half of the photo, he saw his own bottom half. And Joe's. There he was, plowing away at Joe's ass like an overzealous cowboy at an Irish rodeo. His first thought, he never realized his ass was that hairy. He never had much of an opportunity to look at it. His second thought, once reality hit, was that it appeared as though he was shouting "MEATBALLS!" And that's because he was. He remembered it. It was the last time he and Joe had fucked. in his office at the club. Suddenly, he felt dizzy. He needed to go lie down for a while. He didn't even make it through his front door when the lights went out in his head and he passed out on the porch.

"Hey, Dad," he heard his son's voice say.

"Nothing, you?" That didn't make sense. He was out of it. But not so out of it that he didn't have the good sense to stuff the paper underneath his body. That was the last thing he needed his son to see.

Doesn't matter, though, does it? It's in the papers! He's gonna know anyway!

"Shut up! Just shut your mouth!"

"What did I say?" Junior asked.

"Sorry. Go get your mother."

He turned to go.

"No! Wait! Don't get your mother. Just, um, I'll be okay. Really."

"All right," said Junior. "I wasn't really asking."

"Never mind! Go play!"

"I'm hungry. Can I eat some cereal?"

"Yes! Eat some cereal! Go eat!"

Junior turned to go again.

"Wait! What time is it?"

"It's ten forty-five, Dad."

"Ten forty-five? Oh shit. That stupid blond whore is behind this. That bitch is gonna die today. She's *gotta* die."

"Who?" asked Junior.

"Did I say that out loud? I thought I thought it."

"You're scaring me. I'm gonna go get mom."

"No!" He jumped up, still a little dizzy, but

not too dizzy to run to his Hummer and burn rubber out of there. He checked the glove box. The Glock was in there. It wasn't the Smith and Wesson he'd hoped to use today, but it would have to do.

16. The Back Room

He was halfway to the restaurant when he realized he'd forgotten to grab the paper from the porch on his way out. Charlene! It was too late to turn back. If Junior would have just let her sleep instead of rushing in to wake her up, he probably would have turned around. However, he had to keep pushing onward.

His cell phone rang violently. He didn't have to look at the screen to know who it was. Charlene. Right on cue. He hit the IGNORE button. He didn't want to give her the opportunity to leave a voice mail. He would have been too tempted to listen to it while he was sitting there waiting for Blondie.

This was it. He was ruined. He would lose his family over this. His wife may have forgiven him over having a *goomah*, but he doubted it highly. And his *goomah* being a dude? There was no mercy for that one. She would kick him out and never let him see his child again. There was the hope that she wouldn't tell her father. But of course she would tell her father. Jimmy would be ruined. Literally. His only other option was to run. But Don would find him eventually. The old man had his ways.

He pulled up across the street from Rossi's and watched the door so Blondie couldn't go in without him.

His phone vibrated. A text.

WHAT THE FUCK???

Three question marks from Charlene. It was worse than he had expected. There was nothing he could do at this point.

The phone vibrated again.

CALL ME!!! Said another text. There was no way he would do that. He had nothing to say. No explanations. No excuses. He was a cheat, plain and simple. No way he could talk his way out of it.

Another vibration.

UR A FUCKING ASSHOLE!!!!!!!!!

Enough! Jimmy set the phone on the center console and rammed his fist through it. It didn't take much to break the screen, but he kept on punching it. Over and over until there was nothing left but small particles and lots of blood. He was normally one to keep his cool, he had to be, but at that moment he just lost it.

He *was* a fucking asshole. No denying it.

It was time to pull himself together, now. He'd had his outburst, now he needed to clean up and get ready for Blondie to come pulling up. He opened the center console and found some McDonald's napkins to wipe up his hand with. There was half a bottle of scotch in there, too. Probably not as good for cleaning wounds as, say, vodka or gin, with all its impurities, but it would have to do. He poured it on his hand, and it hurt like a motherfucker. Good. He deserved it. The more it hurt, the better.

Blondie pulled up in her car and got out. She didn't look well at all. What was that look? Was she sick? Was that guilt on her face? Well, he was about to find out. He rolled down his window. "Hey," he shouted, "Blondie!"

She turned and did a half-hearted wave.

"Wait up." He ripped up one of his shirts from the back seat, wrapped it around his hand, tucked his gun in his waistband, and got out of the Hummer.

"How you feelin'?" he asked. "You don't look good at all."

"Flu or something. I don't know. Maybe we

should reschedule."

"Nonsense," Jimmy said. "You know what they say about the flu? You gotta feed it."

"That's a cold. You're supposed to starve a fever."

"Bah, fevers gotta eat, too. Come on, I've set up something special for us."

"You have?"

"Sure. Shall we?" He opened the door for her and followed her in.

"Welcome, Mr. DiFrenzo!" Alfonso, the owner, greeted him kindly. There was no indication that he'd seen the morning paper. "And who's this lovely lady?"

"This is, uh... um... Blondie."

"Blondie?" Alfonso asked.

"Marguerite," she corrected.

"Ah, Margarita, like the drink. Very spicy!"

"Say, uh," Alfonso whispered in Jimmy's ear, "A little young this time, hey?"

Jimmy just nodded and smiled. "I was wonderin' if you'd let me give her the full tour. You know, show her the back room?"

"The, uh...back...room?" Alfonso said.

"Yeah. The back room. I think she'd like to see it."

Alfonso had let him use the back room before. Several times, in fact, for business purposes. Two would go in, only one would come out. He was always compensated, of course.

He whispered again. "Mr. DiFrenzo, are you sure? You have never taken a lady into the back room before."

"I just thought she'd like it, is all. Come on, honey. Let's go see the back room."

They walked through the dining room. There were a fair amount of patrons, and Jimmy could see some of them staring and whispering to each other; some were even laughing. He wanted to scream *take a fucking picture,* but he needed to keep his cool.

He led her, zombie-like, into the kitchen, through another set of doors and down a long hallway. At the end of the hallway was a blue door.

"After you," he said, shoving her in.

He turned on the light and in the far corner was an electric chair with straps, covered in the blood of other associates. He led her to it, sat her down, and strapped her in. This was too easy. She wasn't even putting up a fight.

"See, you, little bitch, have been trying to make my life miserable. I didn't know what you were up to, at first. I still don't. But when my boy got kicked out of Catholic school, I knew you had to be behind it somehow. You little fuck, you let the school know my secret, didn't you?"

She nodded slowly.

"That's what I thought. While I appreciate your honesty, you don't get any points for it. Now, this is where it gets fun!" he said excitedly.

"Huh?" she asked, in a daze.

"What's wrong with you, anyways?"

"What's going on?" she asked.

"Shit. You *are* out of it."

He went to the Craftsman rolling tool bench in the corner, and started pulling out power tools. He monitored her, looking for her reaction, but there was none.

Out they came, one by one, electric drill, circular saw, dynamite, reciprocating saw, nothing. It wasn't until he took the jackhammer out that she made a noise. But it wasn't screaming, or even crying. At first, he thought it was crying, because it was a tad on the hysterical side, but she was laughing. He would kill her, torture her, and she's laughing?

"What's so fuckin' funny?" he asked.

"I... I was... ho ho hee.... I was planning... ha ha ha... to kill *you*."

"Kill *me*? Why the fuck would you kill me? I

thought you wanted to blackmail me."

"Blackmail you? Why would I blackmail you? I'm rich. There's nothing I want or need. No, I have been planning to kill you for *years*."

"Why, though? I don't get it," said Jimmy.

"You don't huh? You don't recognize me at all, do you?"

He looked hard at her face. "Can't say I recall."

"Think back. Fifteen years."

"Okay?"

"You killed someone."

"Honey, you're gonna have to get more specific than that."

"Those scars on your hands? The ones you were telling me about the other night?"

"What about 'em?"

"My goddamned *father* did that. And that was my goddamned *father* that you yanked out of his fucking truck and killed in cold blood in the street."

That explained it. "Oh, shit."

"Did you know there was a little girl in the back seat of the cab? Watching the whole fucking thing? I watched it all, you sick fuck. And not a day goes by I don't think about the disgusting shit I saw you do to him. I still get nightmares. I never had the courage to approach you, let alone plan to kill you, but the other night I had a nightmare that was so bad it made my fucking skin crawl just to picture your fat fucking face."

She spit on him. He felt the wad dangle from his chin but didn't bother to wipe it away. He was too busy contemplating what to do.

"Contemplating what to do?" she asked.

He didn't answer.

"Go ahead. Kill me. Get it over with already. I was about to take my life anyway, after I killed you. Life is fucking boring, and if the only thing that provides relief from the boredom is the nightmares. I can do without it."

Well, when she put it that way, it made sense. She was in pain because of him. No wonder she hated him so much. He supposed he could do her a favor and end her life. He wasn't going to make her suffer, though. After a lifetime of torture, she deserved a quick end. He screwed the silencer on his pistol, aimed the gun at her wincing face, and fired.

17. Don Figarazzi

Jimmy got himself a hotel room that day. He couldn't face his family, that was for sure. His life as he knew it was over. At least here he might buy himself a couple days before meeting a fate similar to Blondie's. The mini bar was well-stocked in the room, so he cracked two of the little bottles, turned the t.v. on, and tried to relax.

Around three p.m. the phone in his room rang.

"Hello?"

"Meet me at the docks. Six o'clock."

Don Figarazzi. Jimmy knew he would be found eventually, but he didn't think it would be this quick. The old man never ceased to amaze him. This is why he couldn't run. Don was good.

It was half past four. He couldn't take it anymore. This may have been the shortest wait on death row in history, but it felt like an eternity. The wait was killing him. Jimmy needed to leave now. He'd track Don down and end it on the spot. He chugged a couple more mini bottles, got in his vehicle, and headed to the docks.

18. The Docks

Jimmy pulled up to the docks a little past five. Some shady guys were unloading some shady ships of shady merchandise, shadily. Looked like it was business as usual. Most of the guys were whispering, gesturing, and laughing, much like at the restaurant. He knew most of the boys here, and he didn't stop to chat, or to yell and scream. He headed straight for Don's office. It didn't matter if Don was in the middle of something. He would make him deal with him. Nothing was that important that it couldn't wait.

Jimmy barged right into Don's office; there was no need for propriety at this point. Except Don wasn't there. It was someone else. "Hey, Jimmy."

"Joe? The fuck you doin' here?" Jimmy asked. Then it dawned on him what he was most likely there for. Don wanted to have a "talk" with Joe as well. But why would Don want to kill Joe before he killed *him*? Shouldn't killing Jimmy be the first order of business? Was Don trying to say that Joe was more important than him? He glared at Joe, suddenly disgusted with him. What was that on his face?

"You got a little somethin' there," Jimmy said.

Joe wiped his face.

"No, no. On your chin." He got out his napkin and wiped Joe's chin for him. There was no mistaking the consistency of this glob. It was most definitely semen.

Right on cue, the boss came out of the bathroom, zipping up.

"Don?" Jimmy asked. "What the *fuck*?"

He looked back and forth at his boss and his *goomah* in disbelief.

"You're early," Don said.

"You're fucking my man?" Jimmy yelled at Don.

"No," answered Don. "I'm not."

"Whew," said Jimmy.

"*You're* fucking *my* man."

"Now, wait, Don."

"Now wait nothin'," Don said. "Look, Jimmy, we all got secrets, right? I just keep mine out of the *fucking paper*!" He threw the newspaper at him.

"That wasn't my fault!" Jimmy said.

"Gimme that," Joe said, and grabbed the paper from the floor.

"Oh, shit," Joe said.

"Jimmy, Jimmy, Jimmy," Don said, "You know it's a rule. You don't steal another man's whore." He aimed his gun at Joe. "And you. You cheating piece of shit," he said, and fired. Joe dropped dead.

"And as for you. You're fired. Your cousin Donald is gonna take your place."

"Oh" Jimmy said. "Hold on. Does this mean you're gonna let me go?"

Don shook his head. "No, you're still a dead man," he said. "But you're also fired."

"Oh,"

"See, you brought disgrace to the Family. The whole fuckin' world knows what you did. I can't just let you go. How would it look for me? Plus," said Don, a tear in his eye as he aimed his gun once more, this time at Jimmy's head, "you broke my daughter's heart."

THE END

I hope you enjoyed B is for Bear.

You like fairy tales? You like them twisted? Check out this excerpt from C is for Cookie.

The old man sat in the living room, whittling and watching *Cargo Wars* on the television, only halfway paying attention to the knife as it missed the knob of wood he was working on and flayed his hand wide open. His wife and two grown children laughed loud and heartily as he bled out all over the room, staining the already heavily-stained couch.

"Haha, good one, Dad. You did it again!" His twenty-six-year-old boy, Hansel, chuckled.

"Yer dumb!" Said his twenty-four-year-old daughter, Gretel.

His glare said it all. Not impressed. "Somebody get me a goddamned rag!" The old man yelled.

The wife rushed out of the room, hurrying back with a roll of paper towels.

"I said a rag, you ninny! Something to stop the bleeding!"

"Oh, you'll be fine, dear. This happens every night."

It was true. It happened every night, like clockwork.

"Yet you continue to whittle," the wife said.

It was true. He did continue to whittle every night, like clockwork.

"Why don't you give it up, Dad?" Gretel asked.

"Because," said the father, "It's my job."

"Your job?" asked the wife. "You've been doing this for years and years and you haven't sold one yet. This place just keeps on piling up with your little carvings. Have you seen the spare bedroom lately? We can't have anyone over for drinks and give them a place to sleep; you can't even see the bed. You can barely open the door. It's chock-full of the little nothings you've created. I don't even know what they're supposed to be." She held up the piece he had been working on. "I mean, look at this. What is this?"

"It's a battleship."

"A battleship? It looks like the complete opposite of a battleship. If someone asked me to carve the complete opposite of a battleship, this is most likely what I'd come up with. You've been doing this long enough, honey. You should have honed your skill. Instead, you've gotten worse since the beginning."

"That's because I keep cutting myself!" he answered. "I have no feeling in my left hand."

"Maybe you should get a real job, Dad," Hansel suggested.

"Yeah," Gretel agreed.

"Maybe *I* should get a real job? Maybe *I* should get a real job?"

"Yes," said Hansel. "A real job. How do you expect to support us with those shitty wood carvings nobody wants to buy?"

"Support you?" the old man said. "Support you? You're adults! Why am I still trying to support you?"

"'Cause we're your kids, Dad," Gretel said.

"Yeah, well, that's up for debate still." He rolled his eyes at his wife. "Hey, here's a novel idea. Why don't *you two* get jobs?"

Hansel and Gretel looked at each other for a few seconds, then a rather large guffaw escaped the both of them. "Hahaha!" said Hansel. "Funny, Dad. Jobs. Ha!"

"I'm serious. I've had it with trying to support a family of four. When your mother gave birth to you two ingrates, I thought after eighteen long years, I'd be finished with this shit. Yet here you are, still."

"That's 'cause you love us," Gretel said.

"Yes. I love you kids. That's why I think it's time you grew up and became respectable members of society."

"But Daaaad..." whined Gretel.

"Don't but Dad me. It's high time you made something of yourselves. You should be out there making your mother and me proud. You should make *you* proud. Don't you want more out of life?"

Brother and sister shook their collective heads. "Not really," they said, in unison.

"You have till the end of the month to get the hell out of my house," said the old man.

"But what are we gonna do?" asked Hansel.

"Yeah," said Gretel. "We have no skills."

A silence fell over them as they all mulled this thought over. It was true. They had no skills. Their attention turned back to the TV, where truck drivers were bidding on long-haul jobs.

"That's it!" yelled the old man, joyfully. "That's what you're gonna do. Long haul trucking!"

The two grown children had another hard laugh.

"I'm serious," the father said.

The silence once again crept in as the children mulled over just how idiotic their father's idea was.

Until the guy with the big beard on TV won his bid to haul a truck full of dwarfs to some broad's castle a thousand miles away. Twenty-six hundred dollars won him the bid, and with that, the children started salivating.

"Gretel, are you thinking what I'm thinking?"

"That our old man isn't such an idiot after all?" asked Gretel.

Hansel looked over at his father and shook his head. "No. He's still an idiot. But even idiots can have good ideas once in a while. Whaddaya say? You wanna do it?"

"Don't you have to go to school for this? How are we gonna afford it?"

"I'll cosign on a loan," said the father. "We'll get you your schooling."

"Really?" asked Gretel.

"If it gets you out of my house, anything."

So they came up with a plan. First, Gretel had to get her regular driver's license. Neither of the kids owned a car, and only Hansel had his license. Any time either of them needed to go somewhere, Hansel would drive them in their dad's old turd-on-wheels. If Hansel didn't want to go anywhere, and Gretel needed to get somewhere, her reluctant father would usually end up taking her, Spoiled brats, it's true; but not for much longer.

ALSO IN THIS SERIES:

A is for Adam

Mailing list

Want to read more? Don't stop here, the action is just beginning.

Go to www.marcrichardauthor.com and sign up to the mailing list to get lots of cool stuff not available elsewhere.

Please don't forget to post reviews. They mean everything to a starving artist. Thank you

Printed in Great Britain
by Amazon